EYE TO EYE WITH DOGS

CHESAPEAKE BAY RETRIEVER

Lynn M. Stone

Rourke
Publishing LLC
Vero Beach, Florida 32964

www.rourkepublishing.com

PHOTO CREDITS: All photos © Lynn M. Stone

Editor: Robert Stengard-Olliges

Cover and page design by Nicola Stratford

Library of Congress Cataloging-in-Publication Data

Stone, Lynn M.
  Chesapeake Bay retriever / Lynn M. Stone.
    p. cm. -- (Eye to eye with dogs)
  Includes index.
  ISBN 1-60044-239-0 (hardcover)
  ISBN 978-1-60044-319-0 (paperback)
  1. Chesapeake Bay retrievers--Juvenile literature. I. Title. II. Series:
Stone, Lynn M. Eye to eye with dogs.
  SF429.C4S76 2007
  636.752'7--dc22
                                   2006012257

Printed in the USA

CG/CG

Rourke Publishing

www.rourkepublishing.com – sales@rourkepublishing.com
Post Office Box 3328, Vero Beach, FL 32964

Table of Contents

Chessies may be more fond of water than land!

The Chesapeake Bay Retriever

Some say that the Chesapeake Bay retriever's closest cousins are ducks! No, the Chessie does not have oily feathers or even a beak. However, it does have webbed feet, an oily coat, and love for water.

The Chessie may not be related to ducks, but it loves to **retrieve** them after a hunter shoots. It is an outstanding retriever for **waterfowl** hunters. In the old days, Chesapeakes used to retrieve as many as 200 ducks a day!

CHESAPEAKE BAY RETRIEVER FACTS
Weight: 55 – 80 pounds (25 – 36 kg)
Height: 21 – 26 inches (54 – 67 cm)
Country of Origin: United States
Life Span: 12 – 13 years

The Chesapeake is less popular than two of its cousins, the Labrador and golden retrievers. Strong-willed and independent, Chessies train well, but not as easily as goldens or Labs. On the other hand, Chessies are the **hardiest** of the retrievers. Their ability to swim in broken ice and against wind and tide is legendary.

A Chessie is large and strong enough to be an excellent goose retriever.

A Chessie plunges through ice to begin a retrieve.

The Chessie, in 1885, was one of the first **breeds** recognized by the American Kennel Club. Chessies are one of the few dog breeds developed in the United States.

A Chessie visits with a young member of its family.

Chessies have great fun on a winter hike with their family.

Chesapeakes, like many other famous sporting breeds, are no longer just gundogs. They are companion dogs, too.

A Chessie trains to retrieve by fetching a rubber bumper.

The Dog for You?

Chesapeake Bay retrievers are loyal, playful, and affectionate with their owners. They are cautious about strangers. In comparison to Labs and goldens, Chessies are more "serious."

Chessies are not overly active dogs, but they are large and athletic. They need outdoor exercise with a purpose. If an owner does not give a Chessie something to do, it will find something to do.

Each Chessie is different. Some are quite content to curl up by the fireplace or on a couch. Others do not like to sit still for long periods.

With proper attention and **obedience** training, Chessies make great pets and housedogs as well as field dogs.

Chessie pups visits a frozen pond with their mother.

Chesapeake Bay Retrievers of the Past

Chessies developed around the shores of Chesapeake Bay, Maryland, in the 1800's. The breed began with the arrival in 1807 of a pair of Newfoundland pups. The dogs were on an English ship that wrecked off the coast of Maryland. As a token of thanks, their owner gave them to one of his rescuers.

*Chessies were developed for hunting in the marshland
of Chesapeake Bay.*

Newfoundland dogs (shown here) were the first of the Chessie's ancestors.

The two pups grew up to be excellent retrievers. They bred with many of the local retrieving dogs. Later, their pups also bred with local dogs. Many of those dogs were mixed-breed, but others were probably English otter hounds, flat-coated retrievers, curly-coated retrievers, and coonhounds.

By the 1880's, Chesapeake area **breeders** had developed the dog we know as the Chesapeake Bay retriever. Chessies are one of the few dog breeds developed in America.

Looks

The coats of early Chesapeakes were dark brown. Today their coats range from dark brown to the color of dead grass, much like the colors of autumn **marshes**.

The water-loving Chessie is one of the first American dog breeds.

A Chessie with a "dead grass" coat cools off in a stream.

A Chesapeake's double coat has a short, somewhat wavy outer coat and a wooly undercoat with plentiful oil. The oil is natural waterproofing. It's an ideal coat for cold weather swims.

A Chesapeake looks somewhat like other retrievers in size and **conformation**. It has floppy ears, a long tail, a deep, wide chest, and legs of medium length. The wavy coat and clear, yellow eyes, however, help identify the Chessie.

After marking where it landed, a dark-coated Chessie retrieves a bumper.

A Chessie stares through golden eyes at the winter marshland around it.

A Note about Dogs

Puppies are cute and cuddly, but only after serious thought should anybody buy one. Puppies, after all, grow up.

Remember: A dog will require more than love and patience. It will need healthy food, exercise, grooming, medical care, and a warm, safe place to live.

A dog can be your best friend, but you need to be its best friend, too.

Choosing what is the right breed for you requires homework. For more information about buying and owning a dog, contact the American Kennel Club or the Canadian Kennel Club.

Glossary

breeders (BREE duhrz) – those who keep adult dogs and raise their pups, especially those who do so regularly and with great care

breed (BREED) – a particular kind of domestic animal within a larger, closely related group, such as the Chesapeake Bay retriever within the dog group

conformation (kon for MAY shuhn) – the desired look and structure of a dog (or other animal)

hardiest (HAR dee est) – able to withstand the most rugged conditions

marshes (MARSH ez) – the wetlands of mud, water, and water-loving plants, such as cattails

obedience (oh BEE dee ents– to obey; to follow commands

retrieve (ri TREEV) – to fetch

waterfowl (WAW tur FOUL) – the ducks, geese, and swans

Index

Further Reading

American Kennel Club. *The Complete Dog Book*.
   American Kennel Club, 2006.
Rayner, Matthew. *Dog*. Gareth Stevens Publishing, 2004.
Kennedy, Stacy. *Chesapeake Bay Retriever*. TFH Publications, 1999.

Website to Visit

American Chesapeake Club – http://www.amchessieclub.org
American Kennel Club Chesapeake Bay Retriever page –
   http://www.akc.org/breeds/chesapeake_bay_retriever/index.cfm
Canadian Kennel Club – http://www.ckc.ca

About the Author

Lynn M. Stone is the author of more than 400 children's books. He is a talented natural history photographer as well. Lynn, a former teacher, travels worldwide to photograph wildlife in its natural habitat.